SNAIL'S SILLY ADVENTURES

SNAIL'S SILLY ADVENTURES

Previously published as two separate books, titled *Snail Has Lunch* and *Snail Finds a Home*

by MARY PETERSON

ALADDIN

NEW YORK   LONDON   TORONTO   SYDNEY   NEW DELHI

This book is a work of fiction. Any references to historical events, real
people, or real places are used fictitiously. Other names, characters, places,
and events are products of the author's imagination, and any resemblance to
actual events or places or persons, living or dead, is entirely coincidental.

ALADDIN

An imprint of Simon & Schuster Children's Publishing Division
1230 Avenue of the Americas, New York, New York 10020
First Aladdin edition June 2020

For information about special discounts for bulk purchases, please contact
Simon & Schuster Special Sales at 1-866-506-1949 or business@simonandschuster.com.
The Simon & Schuster Speakers Bureau can bring authors to your live event. For more information
or to book an event contact the Simon & Schuster Speakers Bureau at 1-866-248-3049
or visit our website at www.simonspeakers.com.
Designed by Karina Granda and Tiara Iandiorio
The illustrations for this book were rendered digitally.
The text of this book was set in Archer Book.
Manufactured in China 0420 SCP
2 4 6 8 10 9 7 5 3 1
Library of Congress Control Number 2019948054
ISBN 978-1-5344-6345-5 (hc)
ISBN 978-1-5344-6344-8 (pbk)
ISBN 978-1-5344-7562-5 (eBook)
This book was previously published as two separate books,
titled *Snail Has Lunch* and *Snail Finds a Home*.

For my adventuresome girls, J and P

CHAPTER 1

Snail lived in a bucket.

7

He loved his old rusty bucket.

WARM IN
WINTER

COOL IN
SUMMER

DRY WHEN
IT RAINS

AND CHOCK-FULL OF
BROWN GRASS AND DIRT

He was so comfy he had no reason
to leave his bucket.

Ever.

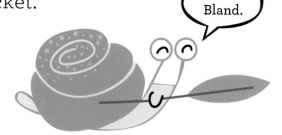

Mmmm.
Bland.

Nearly every afternoon, Snail's friend Ladybug would come by. Sometimes she would tell him stories about her friends . . .

Then Rabbit raced Squirrel to the pear tree, hopping backward.

or stories about the newest
tasty treat in the garden. . . .

You never saw such a huge pumpkin. It was enormous!

And the best news yet! Bluebird said the strawberries are finally ripe.

They are so pretty and red . . . just like me!

Every visit, Ladybug would try to convince
Snail to leave his bucket.

THINKING.

PONDERING.

CONSIDERING.

RUMINATING.

No.

Ladybug was disappointed
and went on her way.

Snail would soon find out.

CHAPTER 2

Snail had no idea what had happened.

Where's my brown grass?

Where's my dirt?

Where's my bucket?

Just then a shadow passed over Snail's face.

He shut his eyes tight, hoping it would disappear.

Arrgh!

Don't hurt me!

Stay away!

21

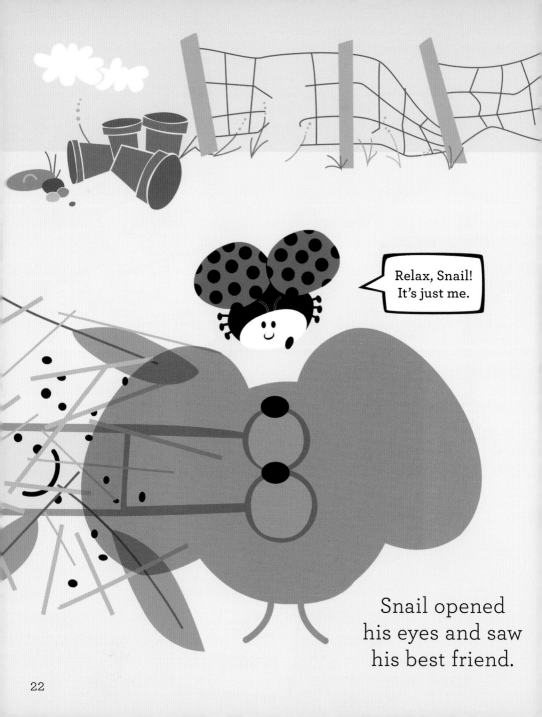

Relax, Snail!
It's just me.

Snail opened
his eyes and saw
his best friend.

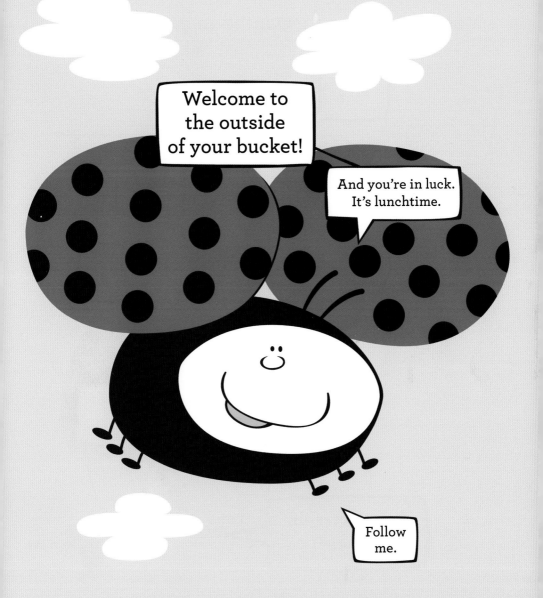

But Snail wouldn't budge. There was only one place he wanted to go: **HOME!**

Snail was scared.
But he was also hungry.

Wait
for me!

Slowly but not so surely,
he followed Ladybug from . . .

some
flowerpots . . .

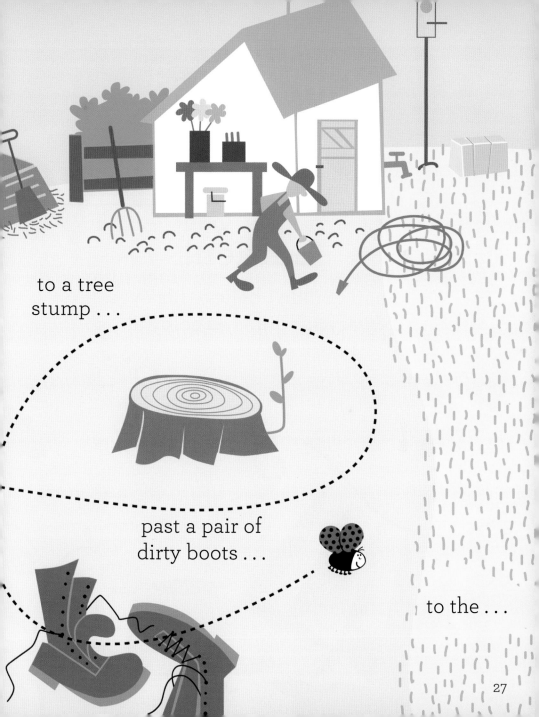

to a tree
stump . . .

past a pair of
dirty boots . . .

to the . . .

27

CHAPTER 3

Garden!

Snail couldn't believe his eyes.
Everything was so colorful.

At that moment a bunch of little red something-or-others caught Snail's eye.

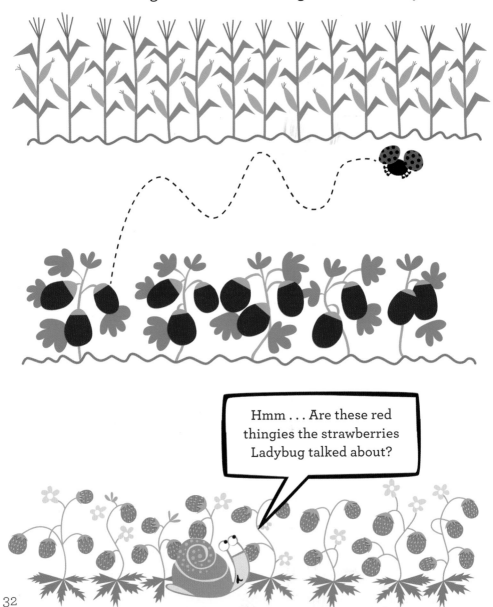

Hmm . . . Are these red thingies the strawberries Ladybug talked about?

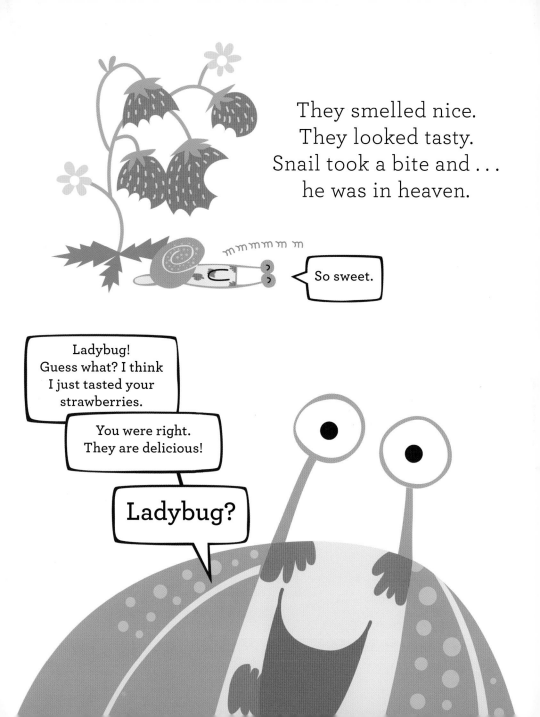

Since this was Snail's first time in the garden, he didn't know Ladybug was only one row over.

CORN

ONIONS

PUMPKINS

OKRA

OT PEPPERS

BLACKBERRIES

RADISHES

SNAIL

EGGPLANT

LADYBUG

CARROTS

GREEN BEANS

Where did Ladybug go?

TRAWBERRIES

CAULIFLOWER

Snail looked
under the
green beans,

Where
is she?

inside the cauliflower,

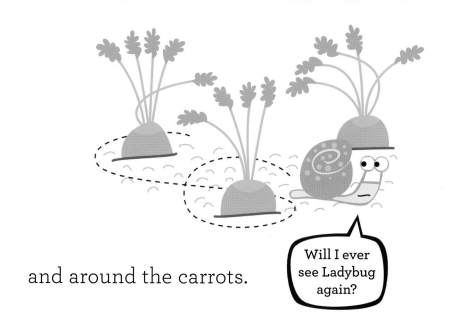

and around the carrots.

Will I ever see Ladybug again?

And then he looked up right into . . .

CHAPTER 4

Two big teeth.

For the second time that day,
Snail closed his eyes.

Snail couldn't believe how Gopher stuffed his cheeks.

When Gopher was finally finished, Snail asked . . .

Have you seen Ladybug?

Never met her.

This wasn't good news.

Well then, Mr. Gopher, maybe you've seen my bucket?

Bucket? Bucket?

Hey, Rabbit! Have you seen this kid's bucket?

Snail looked past Gopher and saw another furry creature. This one was bigger and had long ears.

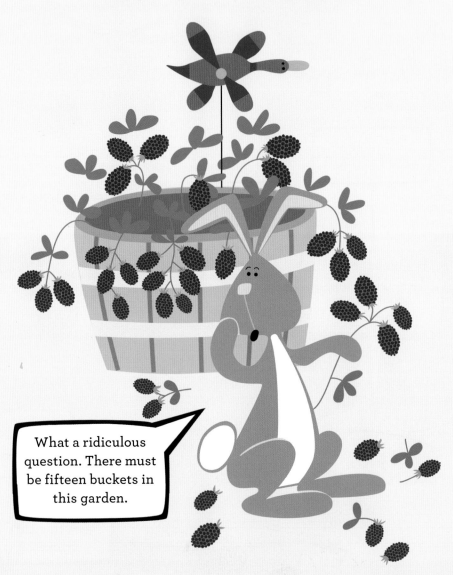

What a ridiculous question. There must be fifteen buckets in this garden.

BIG ROUND ORANGE BUCKET

SMALL RED BUCKET WITH A HOLE

STORAGE BUCKET WITH A SNAP LID

USED PAINT BUCKET

WOODEN WATER BUCKET

OLD RUSTY BUCKET

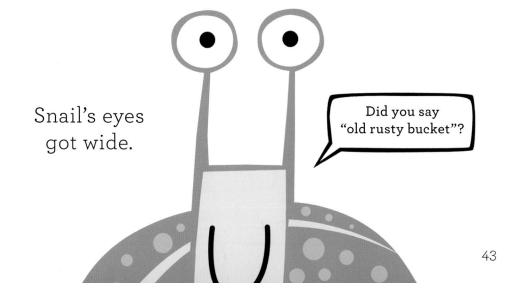

Snail's eyes got wide.

Did you say "old rusty bucket"?

Rabbit took a bite from a blackberry.

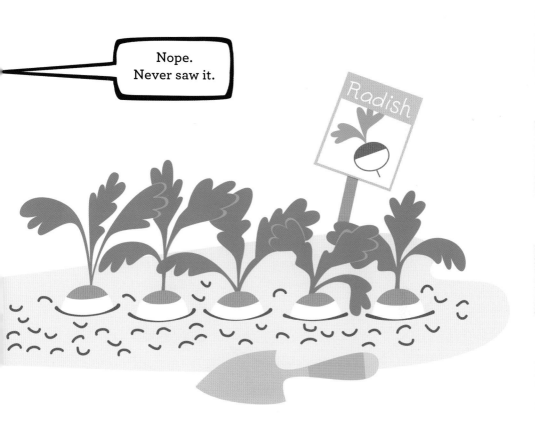

Snail was about to cry.

It's just past the pumpkins. I'll take you there after this last bite.

Snail grinned from eyeball to eyeball.

Soon he would be home. And he hoped Ladybug would be there waiting for him.

47

CHAPTER 5

When Rabbit finished his blackberries, he quickly led the way. Snail moved as fast as he could, but he was a snail, after all.

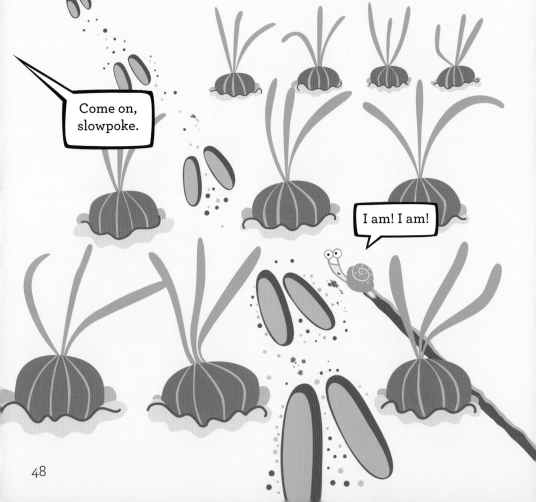

Right past the onions, another pretty
little red strawberry appeared in front of him.

Just one more taste,
and I'll hurry home.

Now, if Snail had ever left his cozy little bucket,
he would have known that was not a
sweet and delicious strawberry.

What he was about to eat . . .

was a pretty little RED HOT PEPPER.

Snail was not happy.

Ladybug was shocked.

Maybe Ladybug had a point. Snail looked dreamily toward the strawberry patch and couldn't believe his eyes.

Ladybug, LOOK! There's my bucket!

Snail and
Ladybug climbe
on Rabbit's
back . . .

and in one,

two,

three hops,

they were at the bucket.

Snail was confused.
The bucket was old and
rusty, but it was filled with
STRAWBERRIES!

Wait a minute.
Whose bucket is this?

It's yours, silly.

64

Oh, Snail!

CHAPTER 6

Now, as much as Snail loved
his old rusty bucket . . .

he loved strawberries even more.
Day after day, he ate strawberries
for all his meals.

BREAKFAST

LUNCH

SUPPER

AND DESSERT

Every day, Snail's best friend,
Ladybug, came to visit. And every day,
she would ask the same question.

Ladybug was always trying to convince Snail that he couldn't live in a rusty bucket eating strawberries forever.

I found some cute homes for you near my house. How about we check them out?

Why?
I have everything I love right here.

Sweet red strawberries in an old rusty bucket.

Ladybug left disappointed.
But she was not a quitter.
Tomorrow she would try again.

The next day, as usual, Ladybug was back. And she couldn't believe her eyes. Snail had eaten so many sweet **RED** strawberries, he had turned **GREEN**.

My tummy hurts.

Before Snail could answer . . .

he threw up.

Okay, maybe you're right.

CHAPTER 7

Early the next morning, Ladybug met Snail
with a long list of places to visit.

honeysuckle
trash can
birdbath
rock
beehive
ambrosia
apple orchard

I'll be your real estate agent.

Snail followed Ladybug to the top of a fence post. In the distance, he spied an apple orchard.

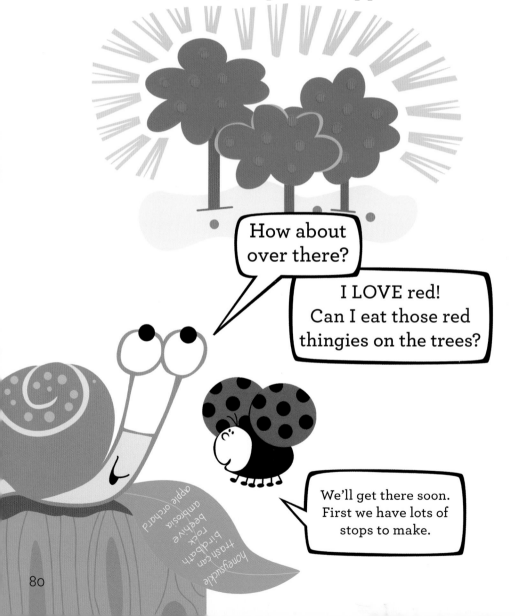

While Ladybug checked her list, Snail slimed down the fence post and . . .

wandered in the direction
of the apple orchard.

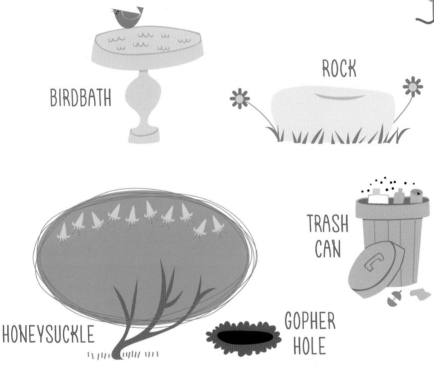

BIRDBATH

ROCK

HONEYSUCKLE

TRASH
CAN

GOPHER
HOLE

GARDEN
SHED

APPLE ORCHARD

BEEHIVE

CHICKEN COOP

DOGHOUSE

AMBROSIA

Now, if Snail had ever seen a chicken or a chicken coop, he would have known this was excellent advice. But he hadn't, so he didn't.

CHAPTER 8

Ladybug led Snail to her
favorite honeysuckle bush.

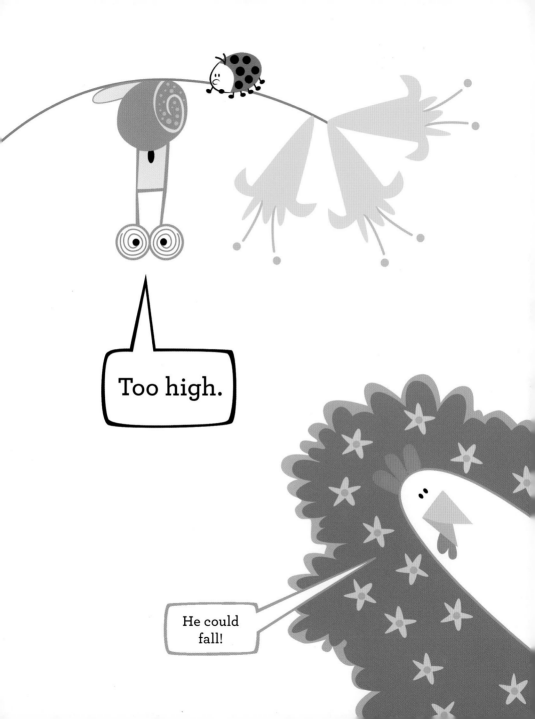

Just then, Snail and Ladybug
heard a familiar voice.

Good morning, friends.
May I suggest something
a bit more sheltered?

It's too crowded, Gopher.

And is this even on Ladybug's list?

Not an inch of space.

Ladybug continued to show Snail
the different spots on her list.
Snail continued to find problems with each one.

While Ladybug, Gopher, and Rabbit looked for Ladybug's lost list, pretty red thingies once again caught Snail's eye.

I wonder if those taste like strawberries.

Forgetting Ladybug's
warning, Snail wandered
off in the direction of
the apple orchard.

CHAPTER 9

Suddenly, a fellow stepped onto the path.
His bright red hat made Snail smile.

Hello, Snail.

Hello.
Who are you?

Ladybug and I are dear friends.
She asked me to show you some
other special homes, including
the apple orchard.

Apple?
What's an
apple?

As the search went on
back at Ambrosia Acres . . .

There are lots of great
snacks in this direction:
corn . . .
lettuce . . .
oats . . .

Snail was happy to follow
Ladybug's helpful friend with
the beautiful red hat. They headed
around the back of a little shed.

But when they got to the back of the shed, the fellow in the red hat stopped, causing Snail to run SMACK into his leg.

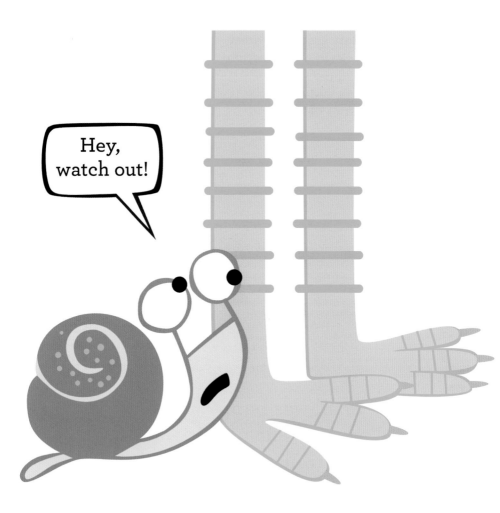

Snail couldn't help but take a close-up look.

YELLOW LEGS

WHITE FEATHERS

POINTY BEAK

Chicken grinned at Snail.

Chicken licked his beak.

Chicken leaned in close.

Thank you for coming for lunch, Snail!

Meanwhile, back at Ambrosia Acres...

CHAPTER 10

Chicken snatched Snail into his beak.

120

Snail couldn't stay
angry for long, because
lying next to him was
a bright red apple
on a pile of brown
grass and dirt.

Snail couldn't
help himself.

He took a bite.

Mary Peterson is an illustrator of many books for young readers, including *Dig In!*, *Piggies in the Pumpkin Patch*, *Wiggle and Waggle*, *Wooby & Peep*, *Snail Has Lunch*, and *Snail Finds a Home*. She lives in Los Angeles, California.